AUTHOR	CLASS
ANHOLT, C.	J

TITLE

The twins, two by two   PARENTS COLLECTION   X

D1325127

THIS WALKER BOOK BELONGS TO:

To Tom and Maddy

First published 1992 by Walker Books Ltd
87 Vauxhall Walk, London SE11 5HJ

© 1992 Catherine and Laurence Anholt

This edition published 1994

Printed and bound by
Dai Nippon Printing Co. (HK) Ltd

This book has been typeset in Veronan Light Educational.

British Library Cataloguing in Publication Data
A catalogue record for this book is
available from the British Library.
ISBN 0-7445-3142-X

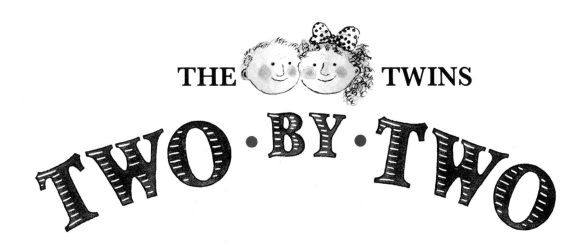

THE TWINS TWO·BY·TWO

Catherine and Laurence Anholt

WALKER BOOKS
LONDON

Minnie and Max were
having a bedtime story.
It was about Noah's Ark
and all the animals.

"Now it's off to bed two by two," said Mummy.

On the stairs the twins were tigers . . .

and in the bathroom they
splashed like crocodiles.

"You sound like two noisy
elephants," said Mummy
when she came up.

"We're not elephants,
we're two little monkeys,"
said Minnie.

"You certainly are," said
Mummy, tucking them
into bed.

In the dark, the twins were
two bats flying.

Then they jumped about like kangaroos.

There was so much noise
that Daddy came up.
But where were the twins?

"We're two little bears,"
said a voice from under
the blankets.

Daddy put one little bear
back in his own bed.

But soon Minnie heard Max crying.

"There's a lion under my bed," he sniffed.

Minnie was very brave.
She looked under Max's
bed. It wasn't a lion.

It was Ginger!

The twins curled up together and closed their eyes.

"We're two little mice," they whispered – then fell fast asleep.

MORE WALKER PAPERBACKS
For You to Enjoy

WHAT I LIKE
by Laurence and Catherine Anholt

"Children's likes and dislikes, as seen by six children
but with a universality which makes them appealing to all...
The scant, rhyming text is elegantly fleshed out by
delicate illustrations full of tiny details."
Children's Books of the Year

0-7445-3019-9   £3.99

KIDS
by Laurence and Catherine Anholt

"From the absurd to the ridiculous, from the real
to the imaginary, from the nasty to the charming, this is a
book which touches on the important aspects of life
as experienced by the young child."
Books for Keeps

0-7445-3011-3   £3.99

THE AMAZING STORY OF NOAH'S ARK
retold by Marcia Williams

"Friendly, lively and intricate... Beautifully coloured borders."
The Observer

0-7445-1469-X   £3.99